Pinocchio

A story by Carlo Collodi
retold by Joy Cowley
Illustrated by Joon-ho Han

Gepetto was a toymaker who made dolls.
One day he made a puppet as big as a child.
"What shall I name this fine fellow?
I know. I'll call him Pinocchio."

The wooden puppet talked and moved.
He acted as though he was human.
He snatched Gepetto's wig and put it on.
Gepetto chuckled, "You are a troublemaker!
I see I'm going to have fun with you!"

As soon as Pinocchio's legs were made,
he jumped up and ran out of the house.

"Come back, Pinocchio!" Gepetto called.

But Pinocchio kept on running.

While Gepetto was looking for Pinocchio,
the wooden puppet went home.
Out of the blue, came a little voice,
"Good things never happen to a child
who doesn't listen to his father."

Pinocchio turned and saw a little cricket.
"I don't want to be lectured by an insect,"
he said, and he threw a wooden mallet.
The poor cricket was killed.

Pinocchio was feeling hungry.
He went out in the rain to look for food,
but no one would give food to a puppet.
He came back and sat in front of the fire
to dry, but he fell asleep by the flames.
His legs were burned.

"Oh Pinocchio!" cried Gepetto,
and he made him new legs.

Pinocchio promised to be a good child.
Gepetto gave him clothes and books
and sent him on his way to school.
But on the way, Pinocchio saw a tent
in the town square. It had a sign:

THE FANTASTIC PUPPET SHOW!

Pinocchio forgot his promise to Gepetto.
He sold his books to get a ticket
for the fantastic puppet show.

The dolls looked like Pinocchio.
"Come and join us on stage," they said.

Pinocchio danced and sang with them
and greatly enjoyed himself.

For his performance in the tent,
Pinocchio received five gold coins.
"I'll buy a new coat for father," he said,
but as he ran home, he met two animals,
a limping fox and a blind cat.

"You can't buy a coat with five gold coins,"
the fox told him. "We know a magic field."

"Yes!" said the cat. "Bury your coins there
and the next day you'll have a money tree
covered with gold coins."

A little voice said, "Pinocchio, they are lying!"

Pinocchio ignored the cricket ghost.
"I'm going to become rich!" he said.

At that moment, two robbers appeared.
"Give us your money!" they demanded.

"No!" screamed Pinocchio.

The robbers wanted the gold coins
but Pinocchio had hidden them under his tongue.
The robbers were angry and tied him to a tree.

A blue-haired fairy had been
watching Pinocchio.
She came towards him,
and Pinocchio began to cry.
He told the fairy everything
that had happened.

"Where did you lose them?" said the fairy.
"I lost them in the forest," said Pinocchio.
Pinocchio's nose grew some more.

Pinocchio's nose grew so long
that it almost touched the wall.

"I'm sorry! I'm sorry!" he cried.
"I will never lie again!

Slowly, his nose returned
to its normal size.

"Where are the gold coins?"
the fairy asked.

"I lost them," Pinocchio lied.
At this, nose grew longer.

On the way home,
Pinocchio bumped into the fox and the cat.
"We've been looking for you," they said.
"We must hurry to bury the gold coins."

They took him to a field and told him
where to bury his five coins.

The fox and the cat said goodbye
and Pinocchio went off to play.
When he came back to the field,
there was no tree full of money.

A parrot sitting on a branch, said,
"The fox and the cat dug up your gold.
You should have known they were lying."

Pinocchio, who had lost all, began to cry.
"What the cricket said was right.
I need to go home to my father."
He hurried home, but Gepetto was not there.
Again, the blue-haired fairy appeared.
"Oh fairy! Where is Dad?" Pinocchio cried.

"He is searching for you," she told him.
"If you stay here, he will come."

"I want to be a real boy and make Dad happy,"
Pinocchio said to the fairy.

She said, "If you are good and obedient,
you will be a real child."

"I will be good. I will! I will!"

Pinocchio returned to school and waited
for Gepetto to come home.

One day, on the way to school,
he met some naughty children.
"Come with us to Toyland," they said.

"What is Toyland?" asked Pinocchio.

"It's a place where you play all day."

So Pinocchio followed the children
to a coach led by donkeys.

For a moment he hesitated and said,
"I did promise the fairy…"

"Time to go!" the coachman cried.

Pinocchio climbed onto a donkey's back.
The donkey said, "You'll be like me.
If playing is all you ever do,
you will turn into a donkey."

But Pinocchio paid no attention to the donkey's advice.

When the children got to Toyland
they did nothing but play all day.
They played ball games.
They rode on toy wagons.
Every single day was fun.

But one day,
donkeys' ears appeared on the children's heads.
They could no longer stand on two legs.
They began to bray like donkeys.
The coachman took them to the market.
Pinocchio, who was now a donkey,
was sold to a circus.

The ringmaster taught Pinocchio tricks.
By being whipped, he learned how to dance,
stand on his back feet and jump through hoops.

But one day, Pinocchio sprained his ankle
and began to limp in the circus ring.

"You are useless!" said the ringmaster,
and he sold him in the market.

The new owner was a man
who made drums from donkey leather.
He tied a rock to Pinocchio
and threw him into the sea to drown.
In the sea, the donkey changed back
and the man pulled up a wooden puppet.
The man was furious. He yelled,
"I can't make a drum out of you.
I'll sell you as firewood."

Pinocchio jumped back in the sea
and a giant whale swallowed him.

It was dark inside the whale
and Pinocchio could not see anything.
"I want to get out of here!" he cried.
"I want to find my father!"

A light appeared and there in the whale,
was Gepetto. "Pinocchio!" he shouted.
"I went to sea searching for you
and I was swallowed by this whale!"

"Dad, I have missed you!" Pinocchio wept.
He hugged his father and they cried
tears of happiness at finding each other.

"We need to escape from here,"
Pinocchio said to his father.
"Dad, climb on my back
and I will swim us out
of the whale's mouth."

When the whale opened its mouth,
Pinocchio caught the surge of water,
and swam out with Gepetto.

"Pinocchio, you saved us!"
Gepetto said, as they came ashore.

From that day, Pinocchio helped Gepetto
and did not miss a single day at school.
One night, the fairy came in a dream.
"Pinocchio, you have become a good child,
Now your dreams will come true."
When Pinocchio woke up,
he was a real boy.
He became Gepetto's true son
and together they lived
happily ever after.

big&SMALL

Original Korean text by Gyeong-hwa Kim
Illustration by Joon-ho Han
Korean edition © Yeowon Media Co., Ltd

This English edition published by Big & Small in 2014
English text edited by Joy Cowley
English edition © Big & Small 2014

Printed in Korea

ISBN: 978-1-921790-44-7